PUFFI]
EART]

Born in Kasauli in 1934, Ruskin Bond grew up in Jamnagar, Dehradun, New Delhi and Shimla. His first novel, *The Room on the Roof*, written when he was seventeen, received the John Llewellyn Rhys Memorial Prize in 1957. Since then he has written over five hundred short stories, essays and novellas (some included in the collections *Dust on the Mountain* and *Classic Ruskin Bond*) and more than forty books for children.

He received the Sahitya Akademi Award for English writing in India in 1993, the Padma Shri in 1999 and the Delhi government's Lifetime Achievement Award in 2012. He was awarded the Sahitya Akademi's Bal Sahitya Puraskar for his 'total contribution to children's literature' in 2013 and was honoured with the Padma Bhushan in 2014. He lives in Landour, Mussoorie, with his extended family.

ALSO IN PUFFIN BY RUSKIN BOND

EARTHQUAKE

RUSKIN BOND

Illustrations by
Sayan Mukherjee

PUFFIN BOOKS
An imprint of Penguin Random House

PUFFIN BOOKS

USA | Canada | UK | Ireland | Australia
New Zealand | India | South Africa | China

Puffin Books is part of the Penguin Random House group of companies
whose addresses can be found at global.penguinrandomhouse.com

Published by Penguin Random House India Pvt. Ltd
4th Floor, Capital Tower 1, MG Road,
Gurugram 122 002, Haryana, India

First published in the UK by Julia MacRae Books 1984
First published in India in Puffin as part of *Escape from Java and Other Tales
of Danger* by Penguin Books India 2010
This illustrated edition published 2016

Text copyright © Ruskin Bond 1990
Illustrations copyright © Sayan Mukherjee 2016

All rights reserved

10 9 8

ISBN 9780143334057

Book Design by Meena Rajasekaran
Typeset in Sabon
Printed at Aarvee Promotions, India

www.penguin.co.in

GRANDFATHER'S BATH

Whenever there was an emergency, Grandfather happened to be in his bath.

He was in his bath when a wild elephant smashed its way through the garden, trampling Grandmother's prize roses and sweet peas and bringing down the garden wall. He was in his bath when the roof of the house blew away in a cyclone. And he was in his bath when a visiting aunt went into hysterics because there was a baby python curled up on her dressing table. On all these occasions he expressed surprise that anything could have happened during the twenty minutes he was in his bathtub; by the time he had dressed everything was over— wild elephant had gone trumpeting on its way, cyclonic storm had passed, and baby python had been removed by young master Rakesh who had put it there in the first place.

Grandfather's bath consisted of an old-fashioned tin tub filled with several buckets of hot water to which he added sprigs of mint. A mint bath! No one had ever heard of such a thing, but Grandfather said it was most refreshing.

Grandfather sang in his bath and splashed around a lot, which is probably why he seldom knew what was going on elsewhere.

He was in his bath when the first shock of the great earthquake shook north-eastern India, an earthquake that was to reduce most of the town to rubble.

The family (or most of it) was living in Shillong, a busy little town in the Cherrapunji Hills, where Grandfather Burman had retired

after leaving the Forest Service. He'd bought a large old house on the outskirts of the town, a house so large and so old that most of his pension was used up in constantly repairing it. Grandmother Burman just about managed to make both ends meet. There were no servants except for Mumtaz, a cook who'd been with the family since Grandfather's forest-service days; he had four small children of his own.

The Burmans' grandchildren lived with them. Rakesh, eleven, rode off to school on his bicycle every morning. Mukesh, six, refused to go to school until he was seven. Dolly, three, followed Grandmother about the house and garden, helping her feed the chickens and the dog (which was half a dachshund and half a spaniel and was called Pickle) and a goat that Grandfather insisted would provide them with milk some day—only so far it hadn't.

The children's mother had died when Dolly was born; and their father, Mr Burman, worked on a tea estate a few hundred miles away, where there were no schools. So the children stayed with Mr Burman's parents, who wouldn't have parted with them for anything in the world.

Every year there were earth tremors in this part of India, but there hadn't been a really big earthquake for thirty years.

'What do you do when there's an earthquake?' asked Rakesh, who had heard all about the last one.

'There isn't time to do much,' said Grandfather. 'Everyone just rushes out of doors.'

'I'll stay in my bed until it's over,' said Rakesh.

'I'll get under my bed,' said Mukesh. 'It can't find me there!'

'It's best to stand in a doorway,' said Grandmother. 'If you look at earthquake pictures, you'll notice that the door frames are always left standing!'

Although Shillong was in a region where earthquakes sometimes happened, the family liked living there. There was a lake and a colourful bazaar, and Grandmother's garden was full of butterflies, birds and exotic orchids, as well as fruit trees and trees that were fun to climb. Rakesh liked roaming around the town on his bicycle. Mukesh enjoyed the sweet shops in the bazaar—when he wasn't wrestling in the dust with Mumtaz's two boys.

Dolly kept herself busy building her own doll's house under the staircase.

Life moved at a gentle pace in Shillong. Apart from the elephant in the garden, nothing very exciting had happened recently to the family. The highlight of the year had been Rakesh's winning the high jump in his school sports, for which he had won a small cup—so small, that he had given it to Dolly to add to her doll's house.

Then one morning, while Grandfather was having his bath, the town seemed suddenly very still and very quiet . . .

THE FIRST TREMORS

Grandfather didn't notice anything because he was splashing about and singing; but Grandmother, who was in the garden trimming her rose bushes, paused in her work and looked up. Why were the birds silent all of a sudden? Not only the birds in the trees, but the birds in the henhouse too. And the goat had stopped nibbling at the geraniums. And the dog, who had been yapping at a squirrel on the wall, sat down quietly, ears back, head between his paws.

'Now isn't that funny,' said Grandmother aloud. 'I wonder what . . .'

And then the opposite happened. The hens began cackling, the dogs barking, and the birds shrieking and flapping their wings. The crows in the neighbourhood all took wing, wheeling wildly overhead and cawing loudly. The chickens flapped around in circles, as if they were being chased. Two cats sitting on the wall suddenly jumped up and disappeared in opposite directions.

Grandmother had read somewhere that animals sense the approach of an earthquake much quicker than humans. And true enough, within half a minute of her noticing the noise

made by the animals, she heard a rattling, rumbling sound, like the approach of an express train.

The noise increased for about a minute and then there was the first trembling of the ground. The animals by this time all seemed to have gone mad and were making a hideous noise. Treetops lashed backwards and forwards, doors banged and windows shook, and Grandmother said later that the house actually swayed in front of her. She had difficulty in standing straight, although she admitted that this may have been due more to the trembling of her knees than to the trembling of the ground.

This first shock lasted only about half a minute, but it seemed much longer. Grandmother realized that Grandfather was in his bath, that Rakesh was on his way to

school, that Mukesh was playing marbles with Mumtaz's son, and that Dolly was under the staircase busy with her doll's house; Mumtaz would be in the kitchen washing vegetables. Grandmother rushed indoors to fetch Dolly.

As she did so, the rumble grew louder. Grandfather did not hear it because he was still singing; but Grandmother heard it, and so did Dolly, who also noticed that her doll's house was beginning to totter. Along with the rumble, Mumtaz heard the rattle of crockery. A teapot slithered off the sideboard and fell to the floor in pieces. In the sitting room, an antique vase (three hundred years old, according to Grandfather) leapt off the mantelpiece and crashed to the ground.

When Dolly felt the first tremor, she instinctively crawled under the well of the staircase, dragging her favourite doll with her. All the doll's hair had long since come out, and so had one eye, but Dolly had had the doll a long time and felt she needed special care and attention. She couldn't understand why the house was shaking, but she wasn't afraid. Houses just shook sometimes, she supposed.

Grandmother did not see her under the staircase and dashed into the drawing room, calling, 'Dolly, Dolly! Where are you?' The clock on the wall went crazy and began striking all hours.

In the kitchen, Mumtaz was trying to catch plates, glasses and dishes as they sprang madly from the shelves. Mukesh had lost all his marbles, and not in a game with his friends. They had rolled out of the gate and down the road and then disappeared into the ground, where a number of fissures had appeared.

Grandfather stopped singing when he found he couldn't manage the high notes. He noticed that his bathtub was almost empty. Surely he hadn't splashed so much! He reached for the mug, but couldn't find it. He started getting out of the tub, but the tub itself rose up and pitched him out on the flooded bathroom floor.

'A ghost!' exclaimed Grandfather. 'There's a mischievous ghost in here, playing tricks with the tub!'

He grabbed his towel and wrapped it round

his waist, then flung open the bathroom door and dashed on to the landing.

By that time the first earthquake tremor was over.

Rakesh was halfway to school when he found his cycle swerving about on the road, out of his control. He almost collided with a bullock cart.

He dismounted to see if the cycle chain had jammed. He found the road as unsteady as the bicycle! But this sensation lasted for just a few seconds. Everything was steady again. Strangely, though, the bullocks were refusing to move on.

'Did you feel that?' asked the cart-driver.

'Yes, everything was shaking,' said Rakesh.

'Was it an earthquake?'

'A small one,' said the driver. 'Or the start of a big one!'

Rakesh rode on to school. The bell had yet to ring for classes, and the field was a ferment of excitement, as the assembled boys and girls stood around in groups talking about the shock that had just been felt. The headmaster had decided that, just in case there was another tremor, the children would be safer out in the open than in the rather ancient school building; and so he delayed the ringing of the assembly bell. Naturally the children were delighted at the delay. But when nothing further happened after fifteen minutes, the headmaster decided it was time for school. There were groans of protest, followed by calls for a holiday. Rakesh was the spokesman for his class.

'Sir, you gave us a holiday last year when the roof blew off!'

'But the roof has not blown off,' observed the headmaster.

'What if the walls fall down, sir?'

'When the walls fall, we will think about a holiday,' snapped the headmaster. 'Now into class all of you!'

EARTHQUAKE GOSSIP

'Couldn't have a proper bath,' grumbled Grandfather. 'There wasn't enough water in the tub!'

'Didn't you feel it?' asked Grandmother. 'Feel what?'

'The earthquake.'

'Didn't feel a thing. You must have imagined it.'

'Well, most of the crockery is broken, as well

as that vase you brought back from Burma. You can eat your lunch out of a banana leaf, or use Dolly's toy tea set.'

'Where are Mukesh and Dolly?'

'Dolly's under the staircase again. It's her favourite place. Mukesh is playing outside with Mumtaz's biggest boy. That tremor didn't seem to bother them. But I hope that shock didn't cause any damage at Rakesh's school.'

'Couldn't have . . . we hardly felt it.'

'You never notice anything when you're in the bath. Everyone else felt it—including the hens! They've suffered nervous breakdowns and won't lay eggs for days.'

Going round the house, Grandmother noticed several cracks in the walls and pointed them out to Grandfather.

'They were there before,' said Grandfather.
'They've been there for years.'

'Well, I hadn't noticed them before. Anyway,
it's time we left this house. It's much too big
and costs too much to look after.'

'I suppose we can settle in Calcutta. But you

won't enjoy living in a small flat. And you're not used to the crowds.'

'I was thinking of another hill station—where they don't have earthquakes. We could sell this place, and buy or rent a cottage in Darjeeling or Kalimpong.'

'Then pray we don't have another earthquake,' said Grandfather. 'No one's going to buy a ruin.'

They heard Mukesh shouting in the garden.

'He's up to some mischief as usual,' grumbled Grandmother, going out to see what all the noise was about.

Mukesh had found a nest and several broken eggs on the lawn, and was shouting because he was being attacked by a pair of angry thrushes.

'What did you do to that nest?' demanded Grandmother.

'Nothing!' said Mukesh. 'It fell out of the tree when everything began to shake!'

'That must have been what happened. But keep away from the nest, or those birds will really go for you!'

The dog Pickle had been running about looking for whoever had caused all the commotion. He and the neighbour's dog began barking at each other, as though laying the blame at each other's doorsteps. 'How dare you rock my house!' they seemed to be saying. Eventually tiring of the argument, Pickle went into the storeroom, looking for rats. He was good at catching rats.

In the town everyone was talking about the tremor that had just been felt. As there hadn't been any serious damage and nothing big had fallen down, it was all thought to have been great fun. But there were older people who remembered the earthquake of thirty years ago, and who had lost friends, relatives and homes when hundreds of houses had fallen down. They knew that a mild earthquake tremor was often followed by a second, more severe shock—and they dreaded this possibility. There was talk of the jail collapsing and the prisoners escaping; of the mighty Brahmaputra river changing its course and flooding the whole of Assam, while crocodiles invaded the towns and villages; of glaciers sliding down from the Himalayas; and of the earth opening up and swallowing the whole of Shillong!

'The end of the world is near!' proclaimed a holy man in the bazaar.

'Tell us, holy one, what should we do about it?' asked a shopkeeper.

'Purify yourself,' said the holy man. 'Take care of your soul!'

'In other words,' said a passing wit, 'don't cheat your customers.'

'And when did you ever work for a living,' shouted the shopkeeper, 'you still owe me twenty rupees!'

Back at the Burman house, the family sat down to a quiet lunch. It wasn't quiet for long, because Dolly wanted what was on Mukesh's plate (even though it was no different from hers) and, when she was told to eat her own food, threw a tantrum.

'These *children*,' sighed Rakesh, bolting down his rice and bean curry. 'It's time they went to school.'

'It's time *you* got back to school,' said Grandmother. 'It's half past one.'

'We're not having school this afternoon. Although we couldn't get an earthquake-holiday, we're going to watch the cricket match. There's a team from Calcutta playing against the Lake Club.'

'Take me with you,' said Mukesh.

'No, you're always falling off the back of the cycle.'

'I'll sit in front, then.'

'You'll stay at home,' said Grandmother. 'The last time you went to a football match, you got lost.'

'But this is a cricket match,' argued Mukesh. 'No one gets lost at cricket matches.'

'Would you like to come with me to the Bengali sweet shop?' asked Grandfather.

'Oh, please,' said Mukesh. 'It's better than cricket. Better than that rotten bicycle.'

'Why do we have earthquakes?' asked Rakesh.

'Well,' said Grandfather, 'the earth has been around a long time—millions of years—and sometimes it feels the stress and strain of being so old . . .'

'Are you a million?' interrupted Mukesh.

'Not yet,' said Grandfather, 'not yet. But, just like me, the earth wants to stretch a little and yawn, and when it does, the earth's crust has these convulsions—we call them earthquakes.'

'But why does it have to stretch here?' asked
Rakesh.

'It can stretch anywhere, and does. Tokyo,
San Francisco, Iran, the South Pacific, Italy,
Turkey—there's hardly a corner of the earth
that hasn't felt an earthquake at some time or
the other. Of course in some places it's worse.
This is one of the places where the earth likes
to do its stretching.'

When lunch was over, Rakesh rode off to the cricket ground, Grandfather and Mukesh walked off in the direction of the bazaar, and Dolly followed Grandmother into the courtyard to help with the washing.

It was about ten minutes later that the real earthquake was felt, and half the town came tumbling down.

EARTHQUAKE CHAOS

Rakesh had almost reached the cricket ground when, all of a sudden, the road tilted and rose up towards him. A second later he found himself sprawling on the ground.

A deep rumbling sound seemed to come from the bowels of the earth, and the road kept

having convulsions. It was like a huge snake thrashing around in its death throes. Rakesh found that lying on the ground was even more difficult than riding his bicycle.

The cricket match, which had started a little while earlier, came to an abrupt end, as a huge

rent appeared across the pitch. Into it fell a fast bowler, an umpire, and a fielder standing at silly mid-on. They were rescued later, but it was the first time anywhere that a match had to be abandoned due to an earthquake.

Those who were playing, or watching from the lakeside pavilion, heard a thunderous roar. It was due to half the hillside falling into the lake. The earth, along with trees, bushes and rocks, simply bulged out, and then came crashing down. Dust and water rose skywards, and at the same time the bed of the lake erupted, rose like a tidal wave and spewed its contents over the surrounding plain. Fortunately for both cricketers and spectators, this massive surge of water was flowing in the opposite direction. But it swept away a number of parked cars, several grazing cattle and goats, telegraph poles, and the walls of the old jail.

Here was a chance for hundreds of inmates of the jail to escape. But they were too shocked by the suddenness of the disaster to be able to do anything except make a dash for the high ground behind the jail. A few could not make it and were washed away by the rushing waters of the upturned lake. Those who reached safety huddled together in groups, waiting to be rescued.

Rakesh saw the wave coming towards him as he lay on the ground. It was about fifty metres away when he scrambled to his feet and ran for the nearest tree. Fortunately it was a large banyan tree, well anchored with its many aerial roots—branches that had come down to the ground and taken root again. It was also an easy tree to climb. Rakesh climbed as high as he could go, glancing down as the advancing water swirled around beneath him. He saw his

bicycle swept past. And he was never to see it again.

Grandfather and Mukesh were in the bazaar, eating sweets. They both shared a passion for gulab jamuns—rose-scented milk and sugar dumplings fried a deep brown. The old man and the small boy stood outside the sweet shop, popping syrupy gulab jamuns down their throats.

The bazaar itself was a hive of activity. It was the busiest hour of the day. The street was crowded with women shopping for vegetables, and pavement-vendors selling everything from shiny brassware to old clothes and second-hand comics, in competition with the bigger shops just off the road. Weaving in and out of the crowd were cyclists, scooterists, pony carts, stray cows, stray dogs and even stray policemen.

Mukesh had eaten four gulab jamuns and Grandfather six when the sweet shop began to wobble about in front of them. Then the cloth awning collapsed, burying the shopkeeper among his sweetmeats. His muffled shouts for help were lost in the noise from the street, where people were shouting and rushing about in panic.

Grandfather and Mukesh found themselves on top of the struggling shopkeeper. As he freed himself, Mukesh got stuck in the awning and had to be helped out, and all the time the ground was heaving about and shops were tottering and collapsing like packs of cards.

In the space of a few seconds, a straight bazaar had become a crooked bazaar. The road had been twisted out of shape to such an extent that some shops that had been on the left now turned up on the right, and vice versa. A beggar in a cart who had never been known to walk now leapt to his feet and ran for his life. The cows had vanished and so had the policemen. A motorcycle had disappeared into a hole in the ground, while a car had mounted the steps of the Town Hall. A tonga pony galloped down the middle of the road; of the tonga and its driver there was no sign.

The Town Hall itself had collapsed, burying a number of clerks and officials. By the time the powerful tremor has passed, several other large buildings had also come down.

Grandfather did not panic. He picked Mukesh off a heap of sweets and helped the dazed shopkeeper to his feet. Then he realized that the earthquake must have affected every part of the town.

'Let's get back to the house,' he said. 'Anything could have happened!'

Grabbing Mukesh by the hand, he started running down the road. Mukesh had trouble keeping up with him. He'd never seen Grandfather running before.

Dolly was helping Grandmother hang out the washing when the shock came. Had they been inside the house, they would not have come out alive.

As in the case of the first tremor, the dog began to howl and all the birds rose from the trees and began circling overhead, making a great noise. Then suddenly there was a wind rushing through the trees, and the ground began to heave and quake.

Dolly looked up to see the tall chimney

toppling off the roof of the house.

'Look, Granny!' she cried. 'The house is falling down! What will happen to my doll's house?'

'Never mind the doll's house,' said Grandmother. 'Let's get clear of the building.'

They ran into the garden just as the walls of the house bulged outwards and the roof fell inwards. There was a great crash, followed by clouds of dust and plaster.

Grandmother looked across the road and saw other houses collapsing, almost as though some unseen giant was blowing them all down. The lines from an English fairy tale ran through her head: 'I'll huff and I'll puff and I'll blow your house down!'

There was a peculiar whistling wind, but it

wasn't the wind that had done the damage; it was the quivering of the earth that had loosened bricks and plaster, beams and rafters. The air was filled with choking dust. They couldn't speak.

How flimsy all the houses seem, thought Grandmother. Just dolls' houses. And yet, many of them had stood for over a hundred years. A hundred years—and in a moment, gone!

The shaking had stopped, but already their home was a mound of rubble. A bedstead poked out of a broken window. A bathroom tap gushed water over a squashed sofa set. Here a bit of broken desk or chair, there a bit of torn carpet, a familiar hat, battered books, a twisted umbrella—these were the only reminders that this had once been a home.

The goat was missing, the hens had vanished. The only things that hadn't been touched were the clothes that Dolly and Grandmother had been hanging up. They remained firmly on the washing line, flapping about in the wind.

Cries from afar came to them on the wind— cries for help, people calling out for each other, some just shouting because there was nothing else to do.

Dolly and Grandmother stood like statues

in the middle of the garden. They were too shocked to move—until they saw Grandfather and Mukesh running down the road towards them. Then they too began to run.

Pickle found himself trapped in the storeroom. He had been ferreting between two large boxes, trying to get at a terrified rat, when the ceiling came down on top of the boxes. There was dust and darkness everywhere. Pickle didn't like it one bit. He wanted to be out of that suffocating hole, and he wasn't going to sit there, waiting to be rescued. The instincts of the dachshund, and his own experience in digging for rats, now came to his aid. He began burrowing in the rubble, trying to tunnel a way out.

THE LUCKY ONES

Mumtaz's hut was one of the few homes left standing. Light and flimsy and made of wooden planks and a thatched roof, it could have been blown away by a strong wind. But it withstood the earthquake. Whereas bricks and plaster had come crashing down, the light wooden structure had shaken and shivered and swayed with the movements of the earth, but it had remained upright.

Dolly was soon at home in the hut, playing on the smooth earthen floor with the cook's children. Mukesh still hung on to Grandfather, while Grandmother, hands on hips, surveyed the wreckage of the house.

'I hope Rakesh is all right,' said Grandfather.

'If you can keep an eye on Mukesh, I'll go and look for him.'

'Yes, do. I'm worried about him,' said Grandmother. 'And we may get another earthquake.'

'Will you be all right here?'

'Well, there's nothing left to fall down. Mumtaz says we must sleep in his house tonight. It seems to be the safest place.'

'You and the children can sleep there. I'll sleep out in the open. It's warm enough—and I don't think it will rain.'

While Grandfather was gone, looking for

Rakesh, Grandmother and Mumtaz searched the ruins of the house, looking for things that could still be used. Unfortunately most of their belongings were buried deep beneath the rubble, and there was hardly anything worth retrieving—just a battered pram, a boxful of clothes, several tins of sardines, some cans of fruit juice that had rolled across the grass, and Grandfather's typewriter, which hadn't been working anyway. They had no idea that Pickle was in the ruined building, buried at the bottom of everything; they thought he was somewhere in the neighbourhood, dashing about as usual, looking for the cause of all the trouble.

'Find my dolls!' demanded Dolly. 'And the doll's house.'

But the doll's house no longer existed.

'No more toys,' said Mukesh with

satisfaction, feeling very grown-up about everything. 'We're poor now.'

'Has the bank fallen down too?' asked Dolly.

'Must have,' said Mukesh sagely.

In spite of Grandfather's prediction of clear weather, it began to rain and they had to take shelter in Mumtaz's little hut. It was very crowded in the small room, but Mumtaz, for one, did not notice—he had a big heart.

The waters of the upturned lake drained away almost as rapidly as they had flooded the surrounding area. Rakesh peered through the branches of the tree in the general direction of his school. He wanted to know the time. Usually the clocktower above the school building was visible for miles around, but now there was no sign of it. It had, in fact, disappeared when the rest of the building collapsed. Even now, frantic efforts were being made to extricate the headmaster from the rubble around his desk, where he had been trapped by a falling beam. The classrooms were a shambles and a fire had broken out in the kitchen and was spreading to other parts of the building. It would be many months before the school would start functioning again. Many would never return to it.

After some time Rakesh climbed down from the tree. He looked around for his bicycle, but couldn't see it anywhere. A lot of other things had been washed up at the base of the tree, including a dead cat, several drowned chickens, fish that had been left flopping around when the water receded, and a cinema hoarding. The face of a famous Bombay film star stared up from the mud.

In the distance he saw a great cloud of dust. He did not know it then, but the dust came from hundreds of fallen or damaged buildings. Rakesh knew, of course, that there had been an earthquake, and a tremendous one, and that it must have been felt over a large area. What could have happened to his grandparents and his brother and sister? He began running for home, taking the road through the town.

He wasn't sure it was the same town he was running through, because many of the familiar landmarks had gone. The town's biggest and most expensive hotel, the Grand Eastern, had tumbled down. Many of its guests had been killed. An ambulance stood in the grounds, and across the road a fire engine was trying to put

out several fires which had broken out. Almost automatically Rakesh began to help the rescue workers who were clearing the rubble. There wasn't much he could do apart from shifting bricks and broken furniture. Then he realized that his own home might be in a similar condition, and he paused, staring horrified at the wreckage of the once-posh hotel. He felt a touch on his shoulder. Grandfather was standing beside him.

'Are you all right, my boy?'

Rakesh nodded, although he looked rather bewildered. 'And everyone at home?' he asked.

'They're all right.' Grandfather did not mention the house. 'Come along, there's nothing you can do here. What happened to the bicycle?'

'It was swept away. All the water came out of the lake. I had to climb a tree!'

They walked home in silence. But all around them there was noise and confusion.

Rakesh hadn't expected to find their house in total ruin. He looked around in shock and dismay.

'Everything's gone,' he said at last. 'What luck—what terrible luck . . .'

'No,' said Grandfather. 'We're the lucky ones! We're alive, aren't we?'

BEGINNING AGAIN

Late that night, Grandfather wondered if he had spoken too soon. There was another strong tremor, and Mumtaz's frail hut swayed and swung as though it were a hot-air balloon. In the town, more buildings came down.

Grandfather had been wrong about the weather too, because it did not stop raining and he had to give up his plan to sleep outside. Everyone else had bedded down on the floor of the hut, using bits of torn carpet and bedding rescued from the house. It was a tight squeeze, with Mumtaz and his wife and four small children taking up half the space, and Grandmother and the family taking up the other half. Nobody slept much, except for Mukesh and the smaller children.

In the middle of the night, Pickle finally succeeded in digging his way out of the ruins.

He was white with plaster, and one of his long ears had almost come off. He sat down outside the hut and howled for most of the night. Other dogs in other parts of the town took up the howling, so it was a weird, frightening sort of night, what with the wind, the rain, the howling—and always the fear of another earth tremor.

Grandfather had noticed that, although the hut swayed about when there was a tremor, it

showed no signs of falling down—unlike the big brick-and-stone buildings that had come down so quickly. Indeed, although they did not know it then, almost everything made of brick and masonry had been levelled to the ground. Wooden structures, no matter how rickety, had withstood the earthquake.

The full extent of the damage would not be known for a few days, because the earthquake had been felt all over Assam and parts of Bengal. A train had overturned at one place, while another left the rails. Over a thousand people lost their lives in the Cherrapunji Hills. The mighty Brahmaputra river burst its banks and many farmers were drowned in the flood. In one small town, two elephants sat down in the bazaar and refused to get up until the following morning. One man was lucky; when the walls of his house came down, a pot of coins showered down on him. But no one else found any treasure.

It rained all night, and although the main shock of the earthquake had passed, minor shocks took place at regular intervals of five minutes or so. Rakesh stayed awake with the grown-ups. He was sure the school buildings had fallen, and there wouldn't be school for months. There wouldn't be much else, either.

Early in the morning, Mumtaz got up to make tea on his small primus stove. Grandfather got up and went outside. It had stopped raining, but even the sky looked wounded as the sun came up red and angry. For many, it would be a long, sad day.

Soon the children were up and playing around the house. Grandmother opened a tin of

sardines—sardine tins were earthquake proof, it seemed—while Mumtaz's wife made chapattis. They went quite well with the sardines. Pickle enjoyed them too. Grandmother had washed and bandaged his head, and he was beginning to feel normal again.

'Will we be going away?' asked Rakesh, munching a sardine rolled up in chapatti.

'I suppose we'll have to,' said Grandmother. 'We can go to Calcutta, or stay with your father on the tea estates.'

'I don't want to go,' said Mukesh.

'Mukesh always wants to do the opposite of everyone else,' said Rakesh. 'What about you, Dolly? What do you want to do?'

'Dig up my doll's house,' said Dolly.

'We'll get you another,' said Rakesh. 'I'll make one for you.'

'It will have to be Calcutta,' said Grandfather. 'There are schools there. Lots of them.'

'No,' said Rakesh. 'We like it here. The school will start again.'

'But we don't have a house now!'

'We can build it again, can't we?'

'Yes,' agreed Mukesh. 'We can build it again!'

'Build it again,' repeated Dolly, 'build it again!'

'All easier said than done,' said Grandmother. 'But where's the money to come from?'

'What's our daddy for?' Rakesh wanted to know. 'He has a job. He can send us money to build a new house, can't he? That's what fathers are for!'

'Yes, I suppose he could,' said Grandmother, opening another tin of sardines. 'That's what sons are for!'

Grandfather was standing at the gate when he saw his friend Azad, the carpenter, passing along the road, looking drawn and pale. Azad raised his hand in greeting and made as if to pass on; usually he stopped to talk.

'What's the hurry, Azad?' asked Grandfather. 'There's going to be enough work in town to keep you busy for more than a year.'

'But for what—for whom?' said Azad, without stopping. 'My wife and daughter are lying in the military hospital—it's the only one left—and I don't know if they will live . . . I'm sleeping there too, as my own house has gone.'

And there were others like him who had suffered greatly . . . Mumtaz brought home an eight-year-old girl, a distant cousin of his, who'd lost both her parents when the roof of their house fell in.

'How will she manage alone?' asked Grandmother.

'I'll look after her,' said Mumtaz. 'I wanted another daughter.'

'It won't be easy for you,' said Grandmother. 'You must let us help.'

'It is God's will,' said Mumtaz. 'He has spared us—we must care for those who were not so fortunate.'

While most of the survivors of the earthquake began leaving the town, Grandfather and his family began the task of putting their property together again. They would clear the rubble, salvage what could still be used and then start from scratch; but Grandfather had decided to use only the smaller bricks together with light wooden frames. 'So that if there's another earthquake,' he said, 'we can sway and rock like Mumtaz's hut, instead of crashing to the ground.'

'I suppose there's something to be learnt from a disaster,' said Grandmother.

A neighbour looked over the broken wall and asked, 'Aren't you people leaving?'

'No,' said Grandfather. 'We're staying.'

'The experts say there's sure to be another earthquake.'

'Who knows?' said Grandfather.

'Don't you believe the experts?'

'Did they predict this earthquake?'

'No, they didn't,' admitted the neighbour.

'So why run away? Where are you off to?'

'Cuttack.'

'The experts predict there'll be a cyclone in Cuttack.'

The neighbour threw up his arms in horror and walked away, looking thoughtful; perhaps Cuttack wasn't such a good idea after all.

Where did one go, in order to escape disaster?

Grandfather and the family had decided to stay where they had always lived and face it out. Maybe there *would* be another earthquake. But they'd be prepared this time. And meanwhile, there were a few compensations. Mukesh and Dolly had recovered some of their toys and dolls, battered but still recognizable; Grandmother's oven had turned up almost intact from the bottom of the rubble, and biscuits were about to be made; and Grandfather had recovered his twisted tin bathtub and hammered it back into shape.

He'd placed it under the mango tree, filled it with hot water and taken his bath in the afternoon sunshine. There hadn't been any soap, but there was plenty of mint in the garden. He started singing at the top of his voice, and the birds, who had just begun to return to the grove, took off in alarm and flew away again.